BEGINNINGS

THE EVENTS IN 'BEGINNINGS' OCCUR WHEN SHINE OF THE MOON WAS STILL A YOUNG VILLAGE GOBLIN ABOLIT TO HAVE HER FIRST REAL ADVENTURE. IT IS SET IMMEDIATLY BEFORE THE EVENTS OF BOOK ONE 'SHINE OF THE MOON'

I WEARY OF THIS IDLE TIME, I'M SO BE BORED, WHAT DOST THOU WANT TO DO?

I DUNNO, WE COULD GO LOOK AT THE HUMANS
WHAT ARE HUMANS?
THEY ARE ODD CREATURES, A BIT LIKE US, NOT AS INTELLIGENT PERHAPS
LIKE TROLLS?
YES, BUT THEY LOOK A BIT MORE LIKE WE DO, BUT THEY'VE GOT FUNNY EARS
HAST THOU SEEN THEM?

NAE, BUT LEAF ON THE WIND SAID HIS COUSIN SAW THEM. THEY WRAP THEMSELVES UP IN BLANKETS ALL THE TIME HE SAID
WHY? ART THEY COLD?
DUNNO
IS IT FAR? I HAVE THINGS TO DO LATER
NOT FAR, ABOUT 40 KS, TWO HOURS EACH WAY
IT IS EARLY, LET US GO

THEY JUST LOOK
LIKE GOBLIN FARMERS
WRAPPED UP IN
CLOTHS
THIS BE
BORING, LET US
GO HOME
THANKYOU FOR
COMING UP HERE TO
PROTECT OUR HOME,
THE BANDITS SAID
THEY WOULD BE
BACK TODAY
WAIT, ANOTHER
HAS ARIVED, SHE
LOOKS MORE
INTERESTING

THEY'RE HERE!
ROOOAAAR
I MUST GO AND HELP
SHHH, WAIT!
ROOOAAAR

SZWOOSH!

I THINK SHE NEEDED NOT THY INTERVENTION. I'VE HEARD OF THESE DOUGHTY WARRIORS, LET US GO HOME IT IS WELL PAST NOON

THAT WARRIOR WAS FASCINATING, I WOULD LIKE TO LEARN MORE OF HER
FARE THEE WELL COUSIN, IT WAS A GOOD DAY
SHINE OF THE MOON! THE COUNCIL WOULD HAVE WORDS WITH THEE!
LOOK NOT SO WORRIED, THOU HAST DONE NO WRONG ... YET!

WE HEAR THOU HAST SEEN WARRIOR OVER IN HUMAN LANDS
YES, SHE WAS DEFENDING THE HUMAN FARMERS
WAS SHE A HUMAN?
I DEEM SO, AS FAR AS I COULD TELL
WE HAVE HEARD RUMOURS OF THIS PERSON, WE HEARD SHE HAD SEVERAL OTHER WARRIORS WITH HER

THOU KNOWEST HOW TROLLS HAVE ATTACKED AND DESTROYED THE GOBLIN VILLAGE AT LAKESEND, WE NEED TO GET PROTECTION FOR OUR TOWN
WE WANT THEE TO APPROACH THESE WARRIORS, RECRUIT THEM, OFFER THEM GOLD!

GREETING HUMAN FEMALE, I AM SHINE OF THE MOON FROM LONGLAKE
WELL MET SHINE OF THE MOON, I AM GRUSHA
I HAVE BEEN SENT TO REQUEST THY HELP AGAINST THE RAIDING TROLLS, WE HAVE MUCH GOLD
GOLD! ALWAYS A PERSUASIVE ARGUMENT
WE CAN COME AND HELP YOU BUT I HAVE TO WAIT HERE FOR MY SISTERS TO RETURN, THEY HAVE GONE TO ELLESWORTH CASTLE

ROOOAAAR!
TROLLS!

ROOOAAAR!

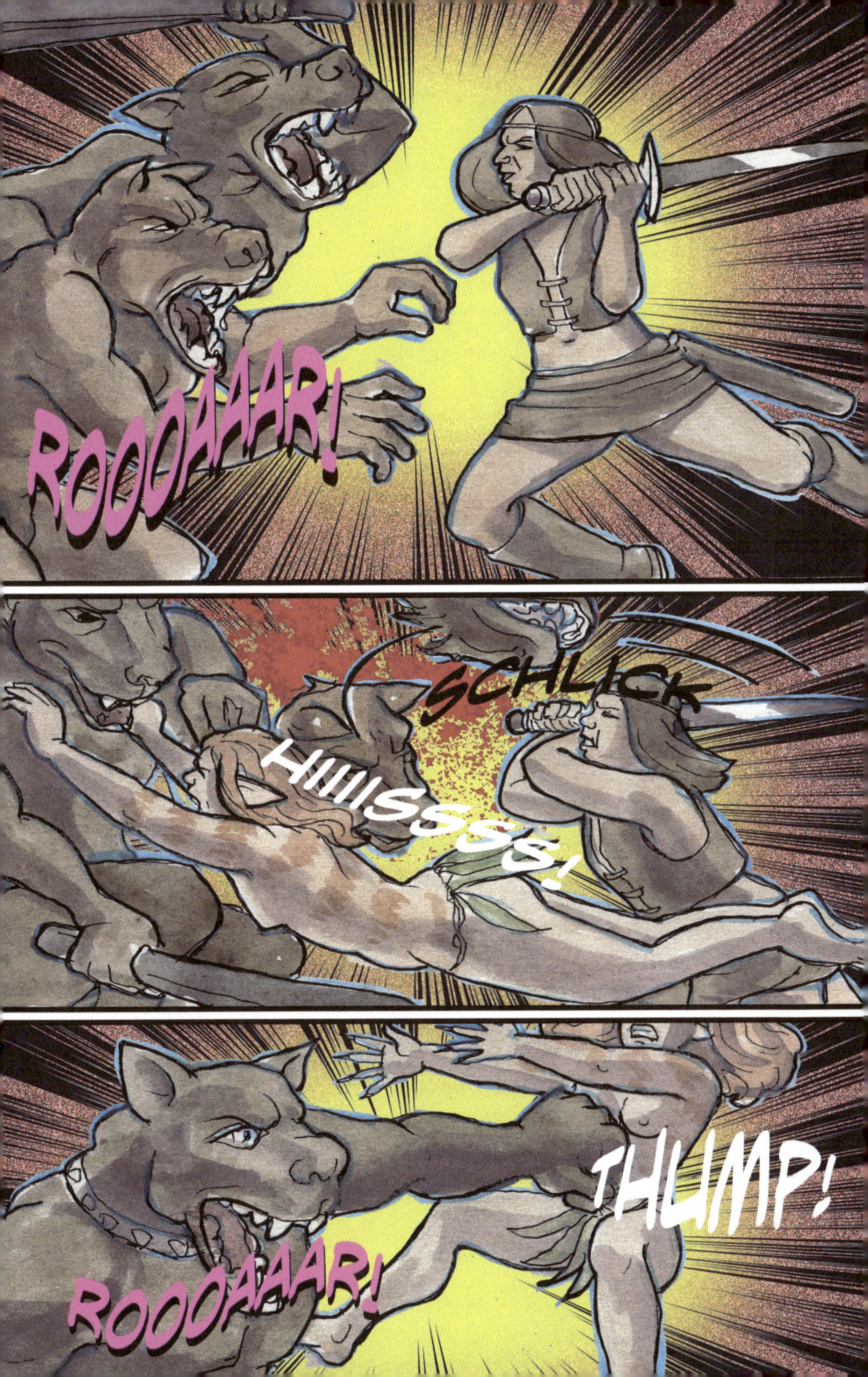

ROOOAAAR!
SCHLICK
HIIISSSSS!
THUMP!
ROOOAAAR!

DIE NOW GOBLIN!
CHLINK!
SORRY FOR DROPPING HIS HEAD IN YOUR LAP, YOU HAD BETTER STAY WITH ME HERE, YOU HAVE A LOT TO LEARN
THANK THEE FOR SAVING ME

THOU ART VERY STRONG AND QUICK FOR A HUMAN
I WOULD LIKE TO FIGHT LIKE ALONG WITH THEE
LET ME SHOW YOU SOMETHING
MY SISTERS AND I ARE ALL HALF GOBLIN
WE COME FROM A MIXED - GOBLIN AND HUMAN TOWN, MIXED GIRL BABIES ARE FREE MARTINS, STERILE, WE ARE TAUGHT TO BE FIGHTERS, TO DEFEND THE TOWN OR TO BECOME MERCS, WE NATURALY DON'T HAVE ANY BACK FUR AND SMALLER EARS SO WE PASS OUR SELVES OFF AS HUMAN

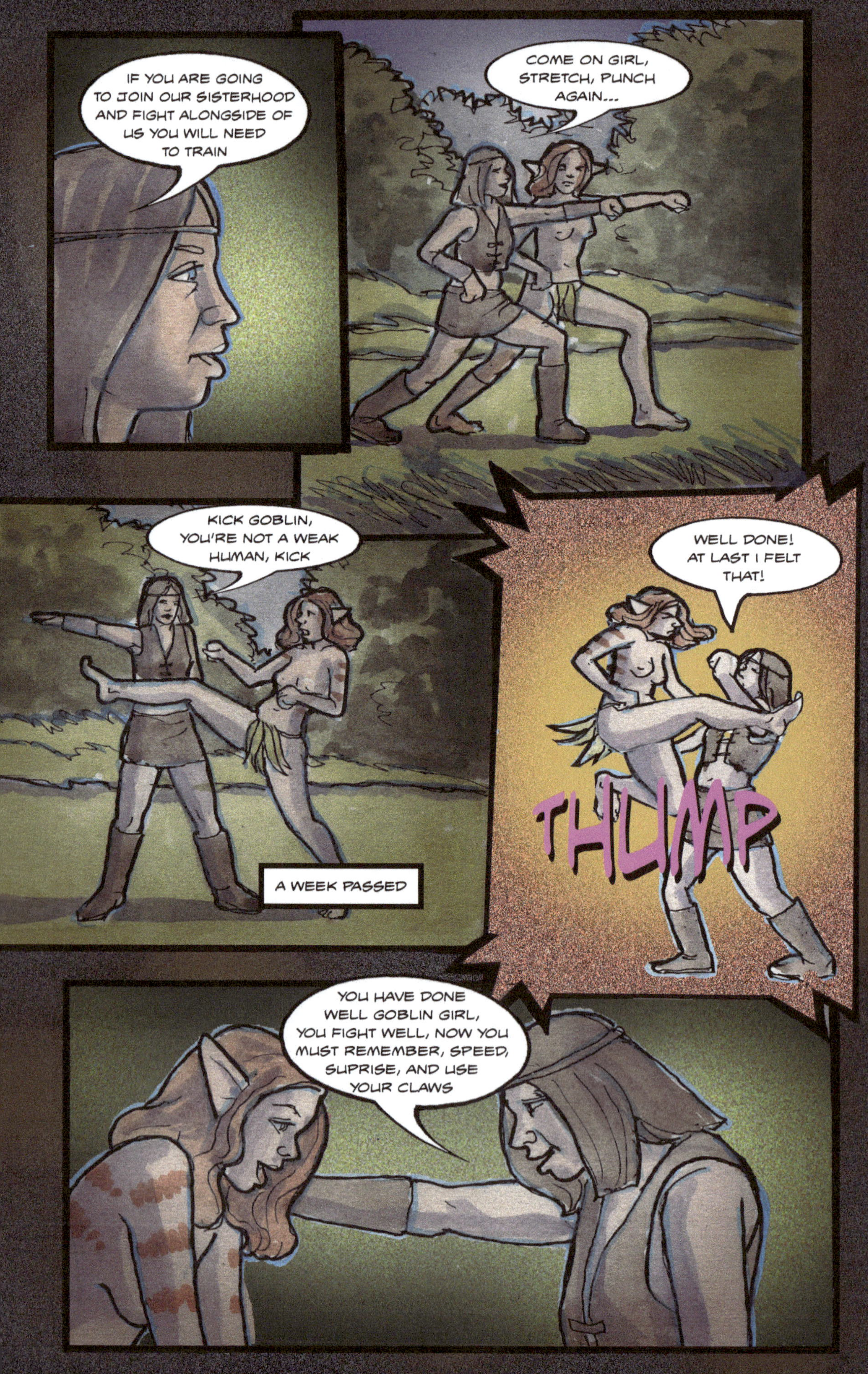

IF YOU ARE GOING TO JOIN OUR SISTERHOOD AND FIGHT ALONGSIDE OF US YOU WILL NEED TO TRAIN
COME ON GIRL, STRETCH, PUNCH AGAIN...
KICK GOBLIN, YOU'RE NOT A WEAK HUMAN, KICK
A WEEK PASSED
WELL DONE! AT LAST I FELT THAT!
THUMP
YOU HAVE DONE WELL GOBLIN GIRL, YOU FIGHT WELL, NOW YOU MUST REMEMBER, SPEED, SUPRISE, AND USE YOUR CLAWS

PRAY, SHOULD I HAVE AN IRON STICK LIKE THEE?
NO, WE HAVE NO TALONS LIKE A TRUE GOBLIN SO WE HAVE TO USE A SWORD
WHY DOST THOU WEAR THE PIECES OF DEAD ANIMAL ON THY CHEST AND HIPS
MY LEATHER GARMETS? WE ALL WEAR SIMILAR CLOTHES IN OUR BAND, IT MAKES US LOOK MORE UNIFIED
REGARD! I MADE MYSELF GARMETS AKIN TO THINE, NOW I CAN JOIN WITH THY SORORITY
NOW YOU ARE TRULY PART OF OUR SISTERHOOD. HOW DO THEY FEEL?
IT IS A LITTLE ITCHY, BUT I WILL GET USED TO IT IN TIME

I REALLY WOULD LIKE TO JOIN THY GROUP, I BECOME SO BORED AT HOME NOW
FIRST WE NEED TO DEFEND YOUR TOWN, THEN I'LL CHECK WITH THE OTHERS BUT I DON'T SEE WHY NOT
HARK! I SMELL SMOKE AND SULFUR?
CRACKLE
CRACKLE

WHAT ON EARTH ARE THESE
THEY LOOK LIKE MONSTERS IN A NURSERY STORY, THEY ARE QUITE CUTE
THEY HAVE COME THROUGH THIS FIREY HOLE IN THE AIR
IT'S SHRINKING NOW, TRY TO HERD THEM BACK IN THERE BEFORE IT'S CLOSED

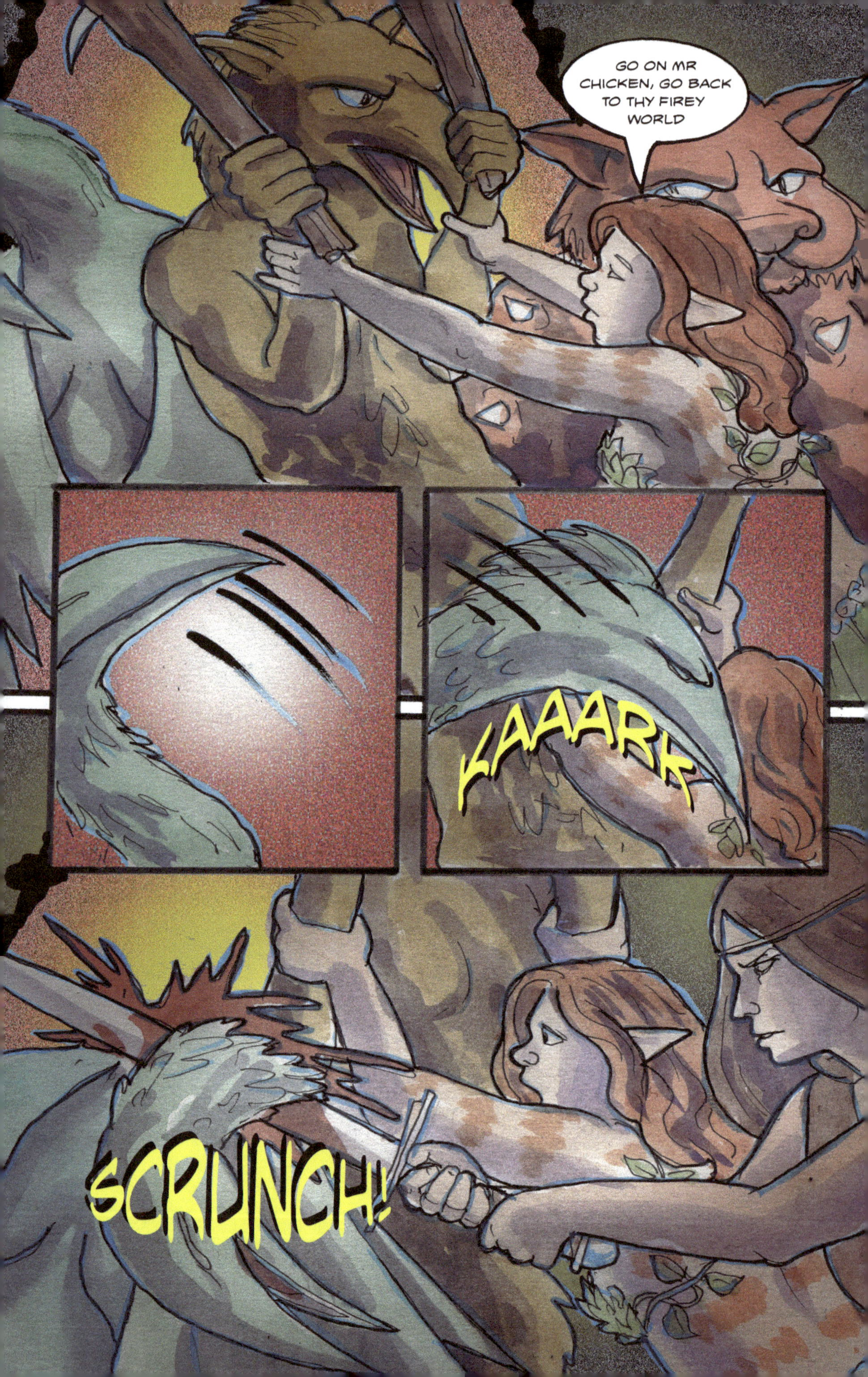

GO ON MR CHICKEN, GO BACK TO THY FIREY WORLD
KAAARK
SCRUNCH!

THOU HAST SAVED MY LIFE AGAIN!

YOU ARE NEW AT ALL THIS BUT YOU MUST ALWAYS REMEMBER...

ALWAYS CHECK WHAT'S BEHIND YOU

UUUGH OH SHIT
SCRUNCH!

I'M SORRY I DIDN'T MEAN TO PROVE MY POINT SO THEATRICALLY.
SHHH, JUST REST, IT WILL BE ALRIGHT...
IT WILL BECAUSE I'LL BE DEAD SOON, DON'T FRET THOUGH, I'VE HAD A GOOD, LIFE
DON'T WASTE YOUR LIFE BEING A SWORD FOR HIRE LIKE ME, YOU'LL BE A GREAT WARRIOR, PUT IT TO GOOD USE, PROTECT PEOPLE. PLEASE TAKE MY SWORD TO MY SISTERS AT ELLESWORTH...
FAREWELL...

GREETING HUMANS, I SEEK THE MEMBERS OF THE SISTERHOOD
THE PATRICIAN WANTS TO SEE ANYONE LOOKING FOR THEM, YOU ARE LUCKY, I'D HAVE JUST GIVEN YOU TO THE GUARDS, I RECKON YOU'RE HUMAN ENOUGH TO ENTERTAIN ALL OF THEM
WHAT? I KEN NOT THY MEANING

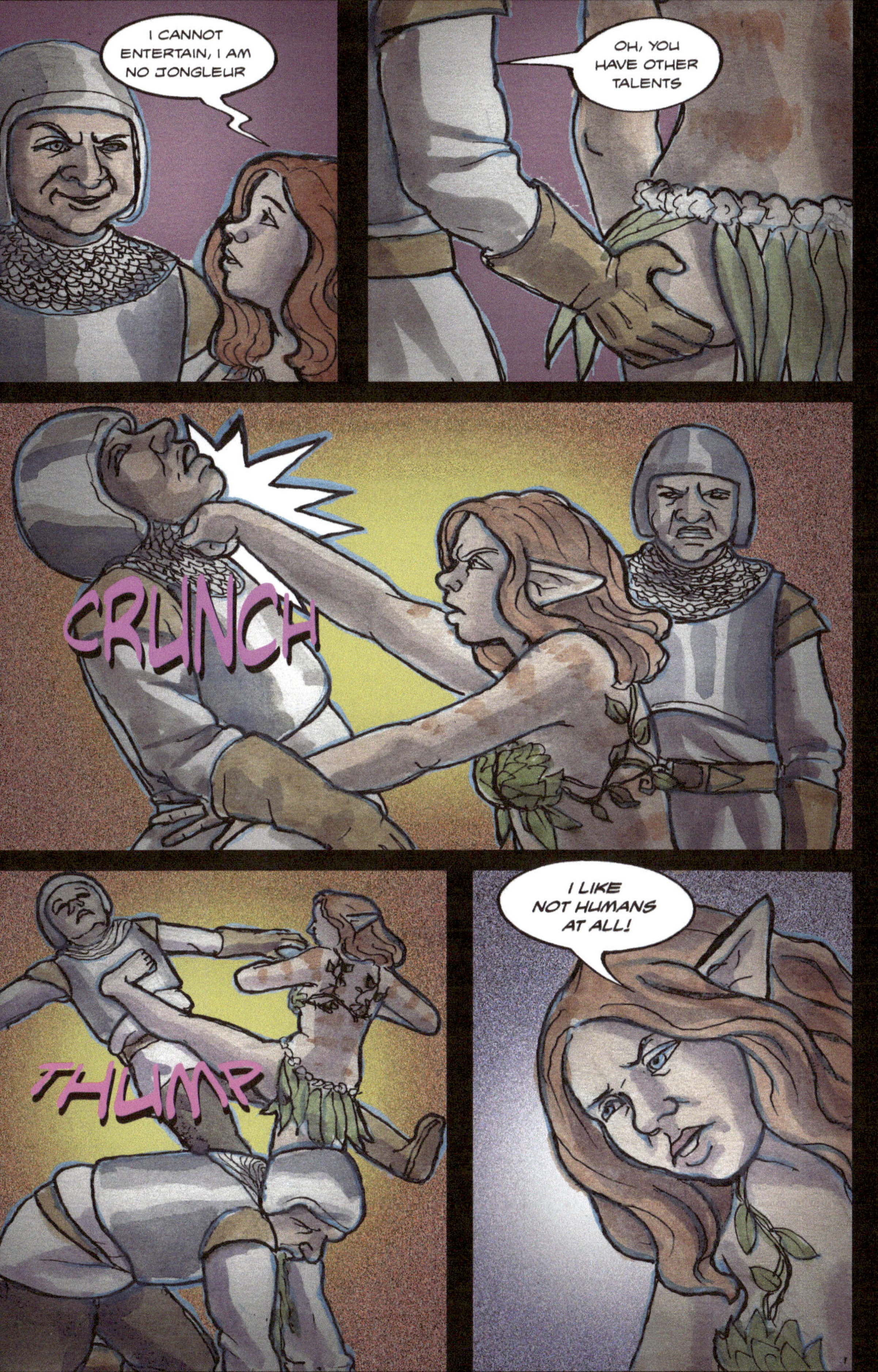

I CANNOT ENTERTAIN, I AM NO JONGLEUR
OH, YOU HAVE OTHER TALENTS

CRUNCH

THUMP

I LIKE NOT HUMANS AT ALL!

EXCESE ME MAAM WHERE ARE THE GUARDS ESCOURTING YOU?
I LEFT THEM ON LYING ON THE STREET MAKING LITTLE BUBBLING NOISES ... THEY WERE RUDE TO ME
IF THOU ART THE ELDER OF THIS PLACE THEN TELL ME WHERE TO FIND THE WARRIORS OF THE SISTERHOOD?
WELL, AREN'T YOU A CHEEKY LITTLE THING, A LITTLE TOO ROUGH FOR MY TASTE THOUGH
TAKE HER TO HER SISTERS IN THE DRAGONS CAVE

WHY DOST THOU HAVE THY GUARDS HOLD MY ARMS? THOU TAKEST ME WHITHER I WISH TO GO ANYWAY
YOU CANNOT BE PERMITTED TO MINGLE WITH OUR GOOD CITIZENS. YOU AND THE WOMEN OF THE SISTERHOOD ARE ABOMINATIONS
YOU WOULD CORRUPT THE GOD FEARING WOMEN OF THIS GOOD CITY .WOMEN HAVE ONLY ONE TRUE PURPOSE, TO CARE FOR MEN, TO GIVE THEM COMFORT AND CHILDREN

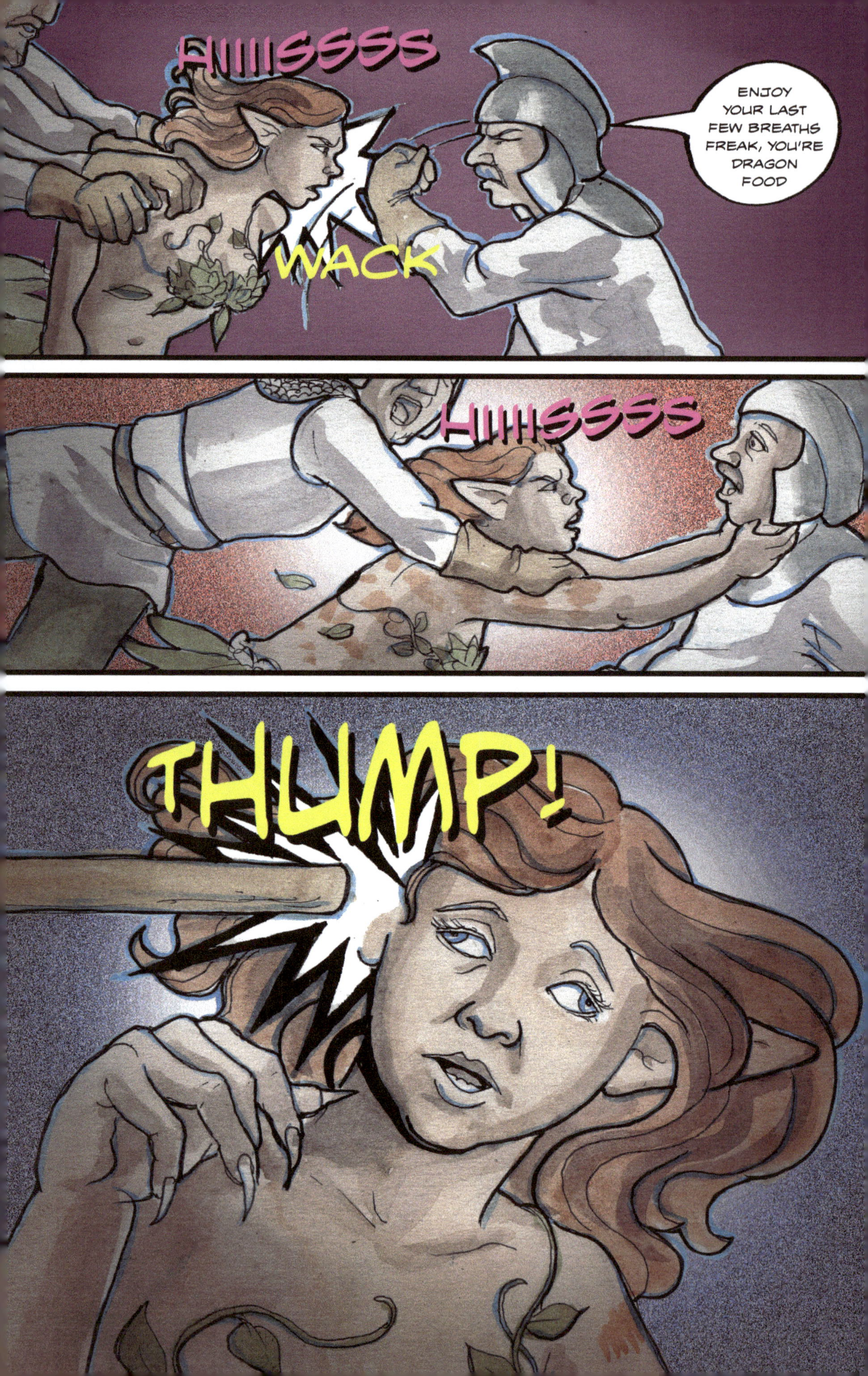

HIIIISSSS
WACK
ENJOY YOUR LAST FEW BREATHS FREAK, YOU'RE DRAGON FOOD

HIIIISSSS

THUMP!

QUIETLY BOYS, WE DON'T WANT TO WAKE THE DRAGON
YOU WERE STUPID TO KNOCK HER OUT SO WE HAD TO CARRY HER IN HERE
NOW RUN!
AH, HELLO LITTLE HUMANS, COME TO VISIT?
ROOAAR!

A LITTLE TOO CRISPY, OH WELL, THE ARMOR GETS STUCK IN MY TEETH ANYWAY

THIS ONE LOOKS GOOD THOUGH, INTO THE LARDER WITH IT

THUMP
OW GRUSHA WAS RIGHT! WATCH BEHIND THEE
HELLO GOBLIN, I'M SORRY TO SEE YOU HERE, SO YOU KNOW GRUSHA?

I'M SORRY, I DID NOT SEE THEE THERE, YES, I KNEW GRUSHA
PAST TENSE I SEE, SO SHE'S DEAD TOO, ITS A BAD DAY FOR ALL THE SISTERHOOD

THE DRAGON CAME FOR US YESTERDAY, WE FOUGHT IT BUT IT TOOK MY LEG AND BOTH OF MY SISTERS
I'M SO SORRY, I HAD GRUSHA'S SWORD FOR THEE BUT THE HUMANS TOOK IT FROM ME
THAT'S OKAY, IT'S JUST A SWORD. I'M GLAD YOU CAME HERE, I WAS GETTING BORED, NOW YOU CAN TALK TO ME AS I GO

THE HUMANS DID THIS, I HATE THEM
NOT ALL HUMANS ARE BAD,, MY DAD WAS A GOOD HUMAN
ESCAPE DON'T DIE HERE...

I WILL SURVIVE

CAN I CLIMB OUT?

OOPS!

THUMP!
OK, SO NOT CLIMBING OUT, I'LL WAIT TO SEE WHAT HAPPENS

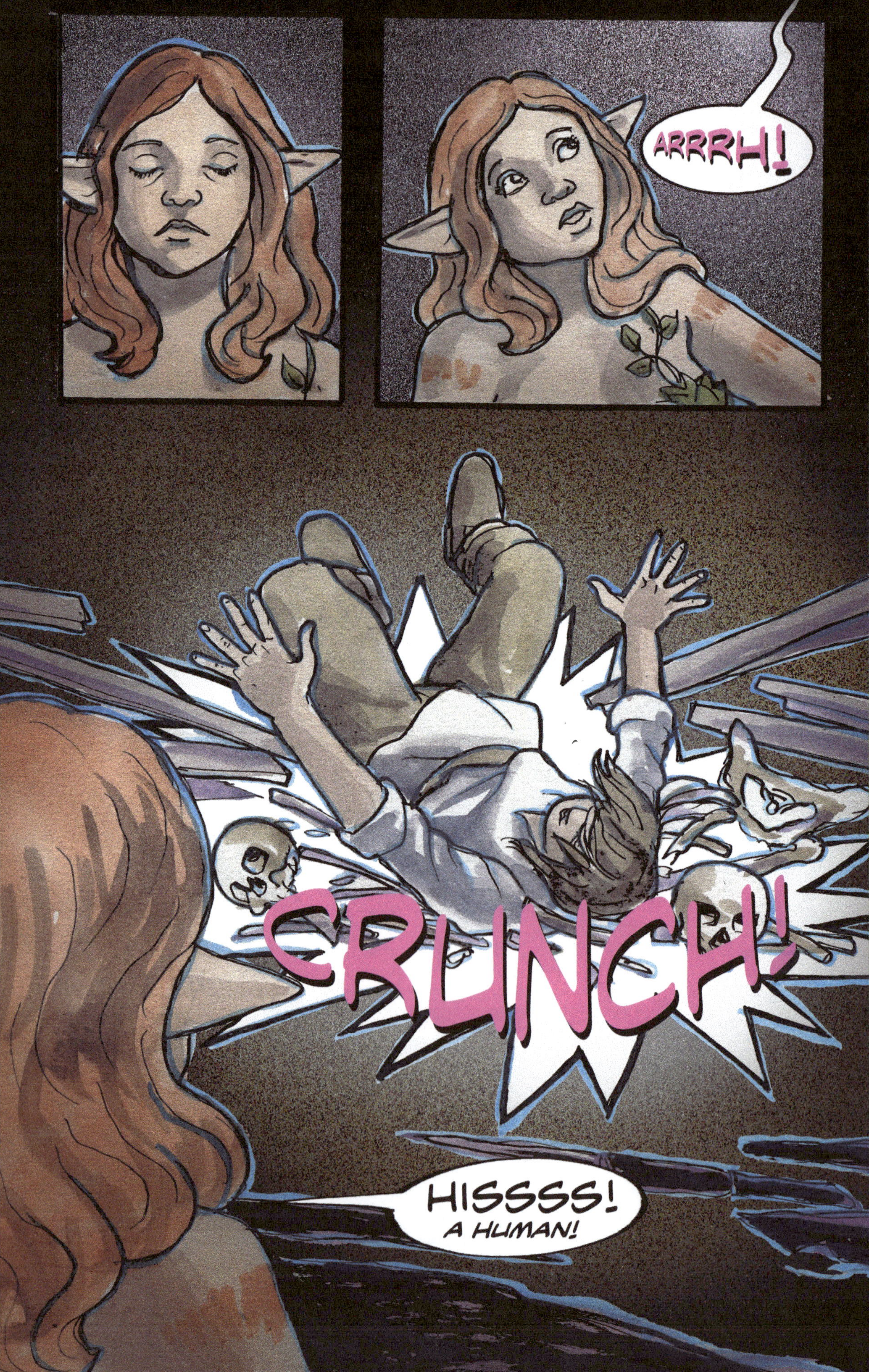

ARRRH!
CRUNCH!
HISSSS!
A HUMAN!

HIIISSS!
HELLO...
MY NAME IS
DALE...
THE STORY CONTINUES IN
SHINE OF THE MOON - BOOK ONE

DESERT DEITY

COUGH
COUGH
BOOM

WHY SHOULD I HELP YOU?
YOU MADE DALE AND I LEAVE
JUST BECAUSE HE WAS HUMAN
WHAT DO YOU WANT?
SHINE OF THE MOON
CAN YOU HELP? CAN YOU
TALK TO THE WIZARD? CAN
HE DO SOMETHING TO
END THIS WINTER

THAT WAS THE OLD WOMEN AND ELDERS... WE DIDN'T AGREE

WHY DIDN'T YOU SAY SOMETHING THEN?
UM.. WE WERE SCARED OF THE CHANGES

TAKE THY DRIPPING NOSES AND GET OUT OF MY SIGHT!... HISSSS

THEY DO HAVE A POINT THOUGH, THIS IS A STRANGELY LONG WINTER
I KNOW.. BUT I WASN'T GIVIVG THEM THE SATISFACTION OF SEEING US RUN TO THEIR BIDDING, BUT YES, LET'S GO SEE THE WIZARD

I'LL LIGHT A FIRE
THESE FOOT GLOVES YOU MADE ME KEEP MY FEET WARM BUT I PREFER TO KEEP MORE CONNECTED TO THE EARTH
THIS FIELD IS IN THE WIZARD'S DEMENSE. WE CAN NOW WAIT UPON HIS APPEARANCE

WHAT ARE YOU DOING?
THAT IS MY WOOD

AHH..WIZARD FRIEND,
I NEED YOUR COUNSEL
OH..YOU...DAMN!

THE PEOPLE AND GOBLINS
ARE DYING IN THIS WINTER!
WHAT HAS HAPPENED TO SPRING?

YOU MUST ASK THE GODS, ONLY THEY CAN CONTROL THE WEATHER
BUT HOW CAN I GET TO THEM
THE TEMPLE WHERE YOU LIVE HAS A PORTAL...USE IT TO TRAVEL THROUGH THE WORLDS

HOW DO WE USE IT? HOW DO WE CHOOSE THE RIGHT WORLD
HMMMPH...WORK IT OUT YOURSELF

GRR.. THOU ART HARD OF LEARNING! THY RETICENCE WILL END IN THY HURT
URK!

THANKYOU FRIEND WIZARD, WASN'T THAT EASIER
SORRY, SORRY... JUST PRESS ALL THE KEYS AT ONCE TO ENTER THE SPIRIT REALM

THIS MUST BE IT
CLICK
ZZZZZ
I KNOW THIS PLACE. THIS IS THE REALM OF THE GOAT MAN
ZZZUMP!

LOOK, THE GOBLIN IS BACK! SHE STILL HAS HER PET HUMAN! ARE YOU LOST GOBLIN?
HE'S GONE NOW, THE NEW HUMAN GODS HAVE LOCKED HIM AWAY
WHERE IS THE GOAT MAN?
I NEED TO SEE HIM, SHOW ME
WHY WOULD WE HELP YOU GOBLIN
HA HA STUPID FAE
SNAP
HISS.. BECAUSE I WILL PLUCK OUT THY WINGS IF YOU DO NOT

CRACK!
THEY HAVE HIM LOCKED IN THE DUNGEON

WHAT DO YOU MORTALS WANT?
I AM THE ONLY GOD! THE ONE YOU SEEK IS A RELIC OF PRIMITIVE PANTHAISM
WE SEEK TO FREE THE GOATMAN GOD

WHAT ARE YOU TALKING ABOUT?
BUT HE IS NEEDED , TO BRING BACK THE SPRING
NATURE! THE GODS OF THE EARTH SEE TO IT'S HEALTH
I'M NOT INTERESTED IN ALL THAT
YOU CAN'T SAY THAT! I WILL SMITE YOU
THEN WHAT GOOD ARE YOU?
TRY! I DONT BELIEVE IN YOU!, YOU ARE JUST A HUMAN DESERT DEITY
WHAT! BUT I HAVE BILLIONS OF FOLLOWERS! IF MY PROPHETS JESUS AND MOHAMMAD EVER STOP FIGHTING, I WILL OWN THE UNIVERSE

HISS.. YOU CARE NOTHING FOR THE HEALTH AND WELL-BEING OF THE WORLDS! YOU ARE A POOR GOD
BOOM
CRACKLE
OOF!
BOOM
HISSSSS

BLAM
SHINE! LEAVE HIM, COME DOWN THESE STAIRS
DALE, CAN YOU OPEN HIS BINDINGS?
...WAIT...YES!
CLICK

SHINE?
WE HAVE COME TO TAKE YOU BACK TO THE WORLD
I HAVE SOME THINGS TO SAY TO THAT GOD FIRST
NOT NOW! THE WORLD IS FREEZING, AND, HE IS MORE POWERFUL THAN YOU
BUT HE IS THE GOD OF HUMANS! THEIR SELF CENTERED BELIEF MAKES HIM POWERFUL. THEY IGNORE NATURE AND THINK ONLY OF THEMSELVES
HOW CAN HE BE? I AM THE GOD OF NATURE! OF LIFE ITSELF!

THIS WORLD IS DYING FROM THE WORK OF MAN! THEIR NEGLECT IS KILLING THE BALANCE OF LIFE!
SNIFF SNIFF
FOR NOW YES, BUT THE PEOPLE MUST LOVE THEIR WORLD AGAIN NOT THAT MONOMANIACAL GOD
CAN YOU HEAL IT?
VERY WELL, I WILL FIX THEIR WORLD FOR NOW, BUT IF THEY CAN'T CHANGE THEIR SELFISHNESS IT WONT LAST. SELFISHNESS IS JUST PART OF THEM AND THEIR GOD!
APEAR BEFORE THEM! HEAL THE WORLD AND SURELY THEY WILL SEE!

WORSHIP NOT YOUR FEEBLE DESERT GOD! WORSHIP ME ~ FEAR ME! FOR I AM OF THE EARTH, SEA AND SKY, I AM ALL OF NATURE!
THE END - FOR NOW

SEARCHING

'SEARCHING' IS SET IN THE NEAR FUTURE, SOMETIME AFTER 'SKYE'S CAVERN LIBRARY' #8 AND DURING THE EVENTS OF 'SHINE OF THE MOON: INCURSION'. SKYE AND KRIS ARE CURRENTLY LOOKING FOR SKYE'S SORCERER PARENTS WHO ARE HIS ONLY HOPE TO FIND HIS WAY HOME AGAIN.

I'M GLAD MAGIC KITTY HAS BLOCKED THE CREATURES FROM OTHER DIMENSIONS DROPPING IN THROUGH THE TELEPORTATION BOOKS ... FOR NOW
YEAH, IT WAS GETTING KINDA SCARY THERE FOR A LITTLE WHILE
THIS IS WHY I NEED TO FIND MY PARENTS AS QUICKLY AS POSSIBLE. LIKE I SAID, IT'S ONLY BEEN STOPPED TEMPORARILY, WHO KNOWS WHEN IT COULD START UP AGAIN
CAREFUL WITH THAT, KRIS. DON'T OPEN IT ALL THE WAY!
SPEAKING OF THE BOOKS, I'VE GOT A LITTLE TIME TO KILL BETWEEN CLASSES. GOTTA FIND SOMETHING WITH A LITTLE ACTION ...
C'MON, SKYE! I'VE HANDLED A TON OF THESE TELEPORTATION BOOKS BEFORE. I KNOW WHAT I'M DOIN'!

FAIR ENOUGH. OH REMEMBER THAT TRIP I TOOK IN THE MEDIEVAL KNIGHTS BOOK A LITTLE WHILE BACK? WHEN I HAD TO RESCUE THAT PET SPIDER OF YOURS? I'M STILL WAITING FOR IT TO DRY OUT. IT'S TAKING AGES.'
THANKFULLY IT'S MADE FROM STAINLESS STEEL, SO IT DOESN'T RUST.
FINGERS CROSSED IT DOESN'T TAKE TOO MUCH LONGER. THANKS AGAIN FOR THAT, BY THE WAY.
INTERESTING. I FEEL DRAWN TO THIS BOOK SOMEHOW ...
MOST DEFINITELY! CATCH YA SOON!
AH, THAT BOOK IS ON MY LIST TO CHECK OUT NEXT. YOU COULD SCOPE IT OUT FOR ME IF YOU WANT.

WOAH, WHAT'S GOING ON HERE?
BLIP!
THAT ELVEN LADY LOOKS LIKE SHE MIGHT NEED A HAND. SHAME I DIDN'T BRING MY MECH ARMOUR WITH ME.
THIS'LL DO!

I THANK THEE STRANGER! I CAN USE THY HAND IN BATTLE!
UH, HEY THERE! I'M KRIS. YOU LOOKED LIKE YOU COULD USE A HAND!

LOOKS LIKE WE'RE TURNING THE TIDE!
WACK
AYE! THE BATTLE DRAWS TO A CLOSE AS THE DOUTY ONES FALL
RIIIP!
THERE YOU GO. THAT'S THE END OF THAT! UH ... SORRY, I DIDN'T CATCH YOUR NAME?!
MY NAME IS SHINE! THANK THEE FOR THY HELP

HIGH FIVE, NEW FRIEND!
STRANGE GREETING, BUT I SHALL SLAP THY HAND!
PAFF!
SHE EXPLODED! DID I SLAP TOO HARD?

PAFF!

I DEFINITELY THINK THAT BOOK WOULD BE A GOOD PLACE FOR YOU TO VISIT!

IT'S FILLED WITH ALL SORTS OF MAGICAL CREATURES LIKE MONSTERS, ELVES ... IT WAS AWESOME! YOUR PARENTS COULD DEFINITELY BE IN THERE.

WELL, AS I SAID, IT'S DEFINITELY NEXT ON THE LIST. GLAD YOU HAD SOME FUN.

RRRRRRRUUUUMBLE
OH DEAR. LOOKS LIKE OUR BRIEF RESPITE IS OVER. THE OLDER BOOKS ARE GIVING US GRIEF AGAIN. GOT A LITTLE MORE TIME TO KILL ... ?
OH NO!

HORSEMEN

THE SHORT STORY 'HORSEMEN' TAKES PLACE IMMEDIATELY AFTER THE EVENTS IN 'THE GOD KILLER' AND ACT AS AN INTRODUCTION TO SHINE OF THE MOON BOOK 16

DOST THOU NEED SUCCOUR? ART THEE ON A JOURNEY?
DON'T WORRY MISS, WE ARE JUST PASSING THROUGH
WE WON'T MAKE ANY TROUBLE, WE ARE FLEEING FROM THE PLAGUE THAT HAS KILLED ALL BUT US
NO NO, THOU HAST MISTOOK ME, WE CAN HELP THEE, COME TO MY VILLAGE FOR FOOD AND SHELTER
WHEN THOU ARE AT PEACE TELL ME OF THY TROUBLES
THANKYOU FOR LETTING US REST AWHILE
THOU ART MOST WELCOME TO LIVE HERE AS LONG AS THY WOULD, THIS HOME IS EMPTY, PRAY BE COMFORTABLE
GREETINGS LITTLE ONE, I AM MOSS ON THE TREE, SHINE OF THE MOON'S AUNT, I LIVE NEXT DOOR, PLEASE ALL COME IN FOR FOOD

WHEN THOU HAST SETTLED IN COME TO THE PUB AND TELL US OF THIS ILLNESS
WILL YOU REALLY LET US STAY HERE? WHAT IF WE BROUGHT THE PLAGUE?
OF COURSE
THEN WE WOULD TRY TO HELP. LOOK, THERE ARE FEW ILLNESSES GOBLINS CAN GET FROM HUMANS
SO THIS PLAGUE SWEPT THROUGH ALL THE LANDS EAST OF THE MOUNTAINS?
YES, IT KILLED EVERYONE IN OUR TOWN, MY HUSBAND WAS A GUARD AND SENT US TO HIS MOTHERS FARM, THAT PROBABLY SAVED US, BUT WE LEFT, I NEEDED TO KEEP THE CHILDREN SAFE
THERE WAS NO WARNING? IT SIMPLY STARTED ONE DAY?
YES, PEOPLE WERE WELL, THEN THEY HAD A SORE THROAT AND IN TWO DAYS THEY DIED, MY HUSBAND DIED

I MUST GO AND FIND WHAT IS HAPPENING
I CAN COME WITH YOU
NAE! I MOST LIKELY CAN'T GET ILL BUT THOU CAN AND I WANT THEE TO BE SAFE

THEY SAID THE FIRST VILLAGE WAS NOT FAR FROM HERE, LET ME SEE

IT IS
AS SHE SAID

BUUUZZZZZZ
BUUUZZZZZZ
BUUUZZ

I KNOW THIS,
IT IS THE BLACK
DEATH, YET SOME
SHOULD YET LIVE,
I WILL LOOK IN
THE CITY

HELLO!
IS ANYONE
THERE?

THEY TRIED TO BURY THE DEAD BUT THEY TOO DIED, THIS IS NOT RIGHT OR NATURAL, THERE SHOULD HAVE BEEN MORE SURVIVORS

IF I FOLLOW THE SMOKE OF BURNING HOMES AND VILLAGES I SHOULD REACH THE SOURCE

BUUUZZZZZ
BUUUZZZZ
BUUUZZZZZZ
BUUUZZZZZZ
BUUUZZZZZZ
PESTILENCE! THIS IS THY DOING?!

THOU MUST STOP THIS!, THOU ART KILLING SO MANY
I WILL DO AS I PLEASE, YOU CANNOT STOP ME, I FOLLOW MY NATURE GOBLIN! DO NOT THINK YOU ARE SAFE I WILL BRING DESTRUCTION TO YOUR COMMUNITY
I WILL STOP THEE
SLASH!
HA HA HA YOU CANNOT HARM ME IN THIS WORLD

HA HA HA
FOOLISH
GOBLIN

NOW TO
MAKE SOME CHANGES
TO THIS PLAGUE SO IT
AFFECTS GOBLINS AS WELL
AS HUMANS AND SEND
IT TO YOUR
TOWN

THIS CANNOT BE
RIGHT! BONEMAN!
WAR! HUNGRY MAN!
I SUMMON THEE TO
STOP THIS DRIPPING
EVIL MAN

STOP PESTILANCE, HE IS DESTROYING WHOLE CITIES AND TOWNS

ZZZZZST!
AT LAST!

THOU HAST COME! LOOK AT WHAT HE DOES, IT CANNOT BE RIGHT

WHAT HAVE YOU DONE YOU FOOL, THESE PEOPLE HAVE NOT GOT TO THEIR TIME
YOU HAVE KILLED THOSE WHO SHOULD HAVE LIVED, I CANNOT TAKE THEM, IT IS NOT THEIR TIME!
YOU DON'T UNDERSTAND, I CAN NOT EVER BRING A REALLY GOOD PLAGUE ANYMORE, HUMANS WITH THEIR MEDICINE HAVE STOPPED ALL THAT IT ISN'T FAIR!

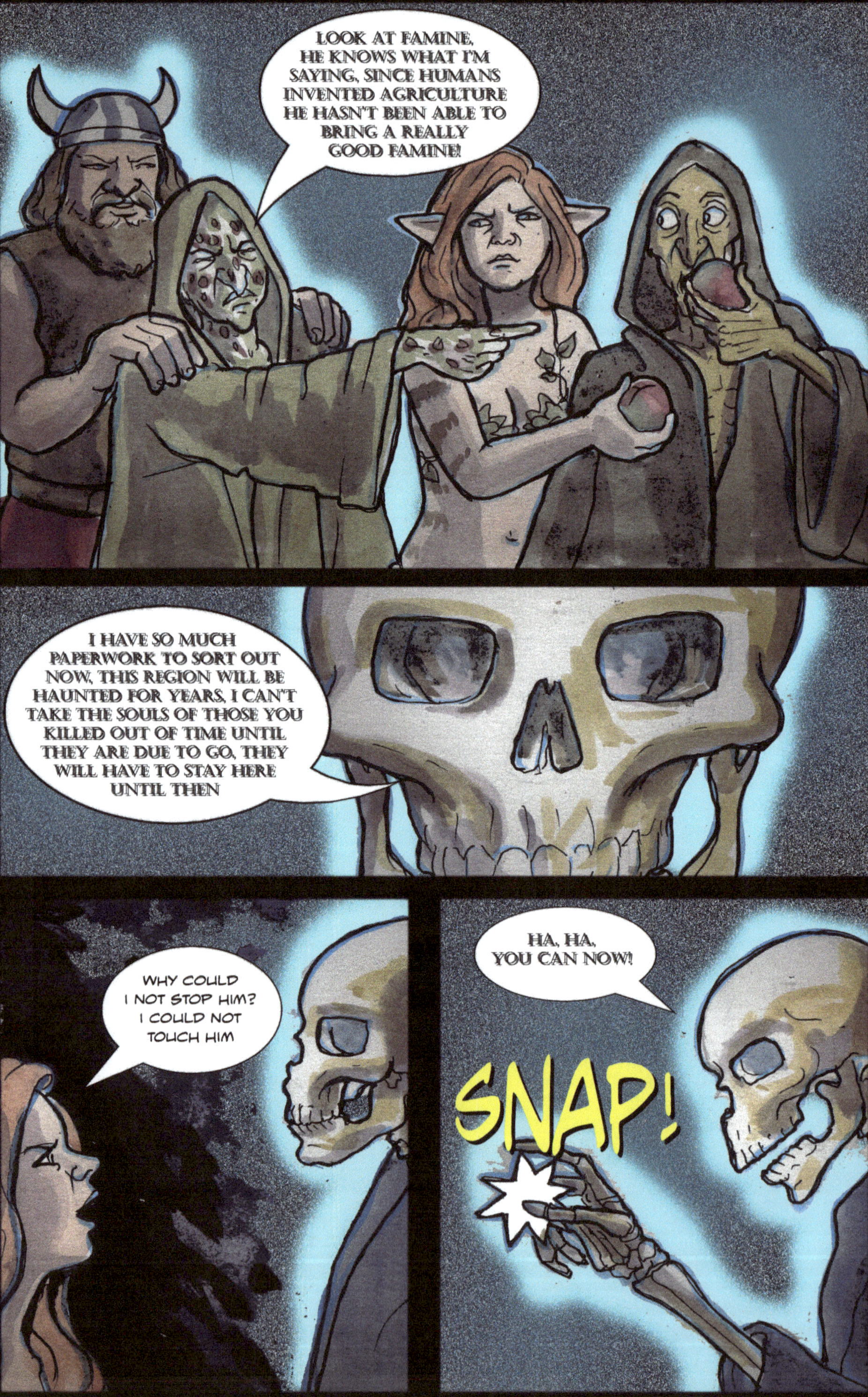

LOOK AT FAMINE, HE KNOWS WHAT I'M SAYING, SINCE HUMANS INVENTED AGRICULTURE HE HASN'T BEEN ABLE TO BRING A REALLY GOOD FAMINE!

I HAVE SO MUCH PAPERWORK TO SORT OUT NOW, THIS REGION WILL BE HAUNTED FOR YEARS, I CAN'T TAKE THE SOULS OF THOSE YOU KILLED OUT OF TIME UNTIL THEY ARE DUE TO GO, THEY WILL HAVE TO STAY HERE UNTIL THEN

WHY COULD I NOT STOP HIM? I COULD NOT TOUCH HIM

HA, HA, YOU CAN NOW!
SNAP!

YOU WILL NOT TRY TO HARM ME, I AM THE GOD OF DISEASE AND DESPAIR, I WILL MAKE YOU SICK
THY ACTS MAKE ME SICK, I WILL TAKE MY CHANCES WITH THE REST
WACK!
HA HA HA

TAKE THAT IDIOT WITH YOU, A LONG WAY AWAY FROM HERE
WHAT WILL HAPPEN TO HIM? HE KILLED ALL THOSE PEOPLE!
I HAVE YET TO DECIDE... I MAY GET A NEW HORSEMAN, SOMETHING MORE MODERN AND TERRIFYING LIKE TAXES OR SOCIAL MEDIA

...AND I'M LEAVING YOU TO TAKE CARE OF THE TWO THOUSAND FOUR HUNDRED AND TWELVE GHOSTS TAKEN BEFORE THEIR TIME. AND THE SIX HUNDRED AND TWENTY FIVE CATS AND SOME DOGS THEY LEFT BEHIND
TO BE CONTINUED

ENDURING

'ENDURING' IS SET WELL INTO SHINE OF THE MOON'S FUTURE. SHINE AND DALE ARE NOW OLD BUT GOBLINS AGE AT A MUCH SLOWER RATE THAN HUMANS ...

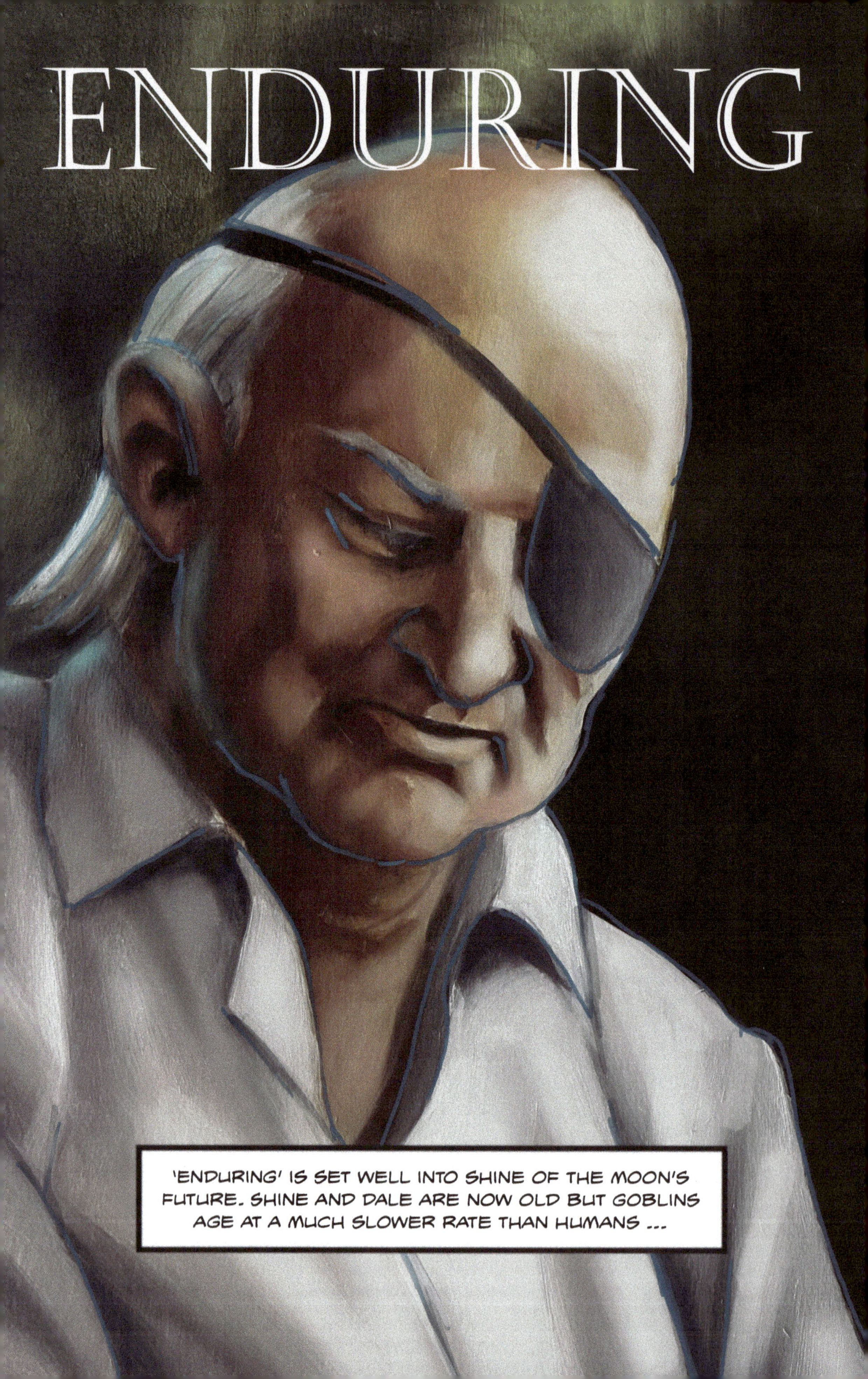

AH SEE YER MOGGIE HAES HUD BAIRNS AGIN
OH AYE, SUM SCUNNER GIT HER UP TH'DUFF THUN BUGGERED OFF

WAS THIS TH'MOGGIE YE TRIED TAE RIDE?
NA, THAT WIS HER GANDMA, AH TRIED AGIN WI' HER MAR BUT NA CHANCE
HOW FUR LANG HAE YE BIN GUARDING THIS WEE LADDIE?
NAE TAE LANG, ABOOT FIFTY YEARS, AH GIVE ME WORD AH WUD MIND HIM FUR HER FUR EVER AND THAT ES NAE YUT
DON BE DAFT, DO VILLIANS TAKE HOLIDAYS?
DO YE GUT WEEKENDS OF?
WHEESHT! SOME ONE IS A COMING

COME ON YE SCUNNER SHOW YER SELF!
OCH AWRIGHT LASSIE
GREETING WEE MAGGIE, DALE SLEEPS?
AYE, HE IS NAE 'ERE AT TH' MOMENT, HIS MYND IS OOT TRAVELIN'
I THANK THEE MY FRIEND FOR LOOKING AFTER HIM WHEN I BE ABSENT
WEE FASH YE NOT ABOOT LIT, I GAV' YE MA WORD

IT BE NICE ANGUS CAME TO SEE THEE, GO SPEND SOME TIME WITH HIM IF THOU WILL, I BE HERE TO LOOK AFTER DALE NOW
WEE OH AYE, JUS KEEP EDGY FUR THAT JIMMY WI' T H' SYTHE
SHINE! YOU'RE BACK!
DALE?
I'M SORRY, YOU CAUGHT ME NAPPING, IT'S SO GOOD TO SEE YOU

COME IN COME IN, I'LL COOK DINNER
SORRY, MY MEMORY'S A BIT FUZZY, WHAT DID YOU DO TODAY?
I HAD TO GO HELP THE MASONS OVER AT ELLSWORTH CASTLE, THOU REMEMBERS THEY STARTED REBUILDING

A GROUP OF SEAFARING NOMADS ARRIVED AND WANTED TO TAKE OVER THE TOWN

THEY HAD LOST THEIR LAND IN THE HEATING OF THE WORLD AND HAD BEEN HOMELESS SINCE. THEY SAID BECAUSE ONE OF THEIR ANCESTORS HAD BEEN THE EXPLORER WHO NAMED THIS AREA, THEY HAD THE RIGHT TO TAKE IT FROM ITS INHABITANTS

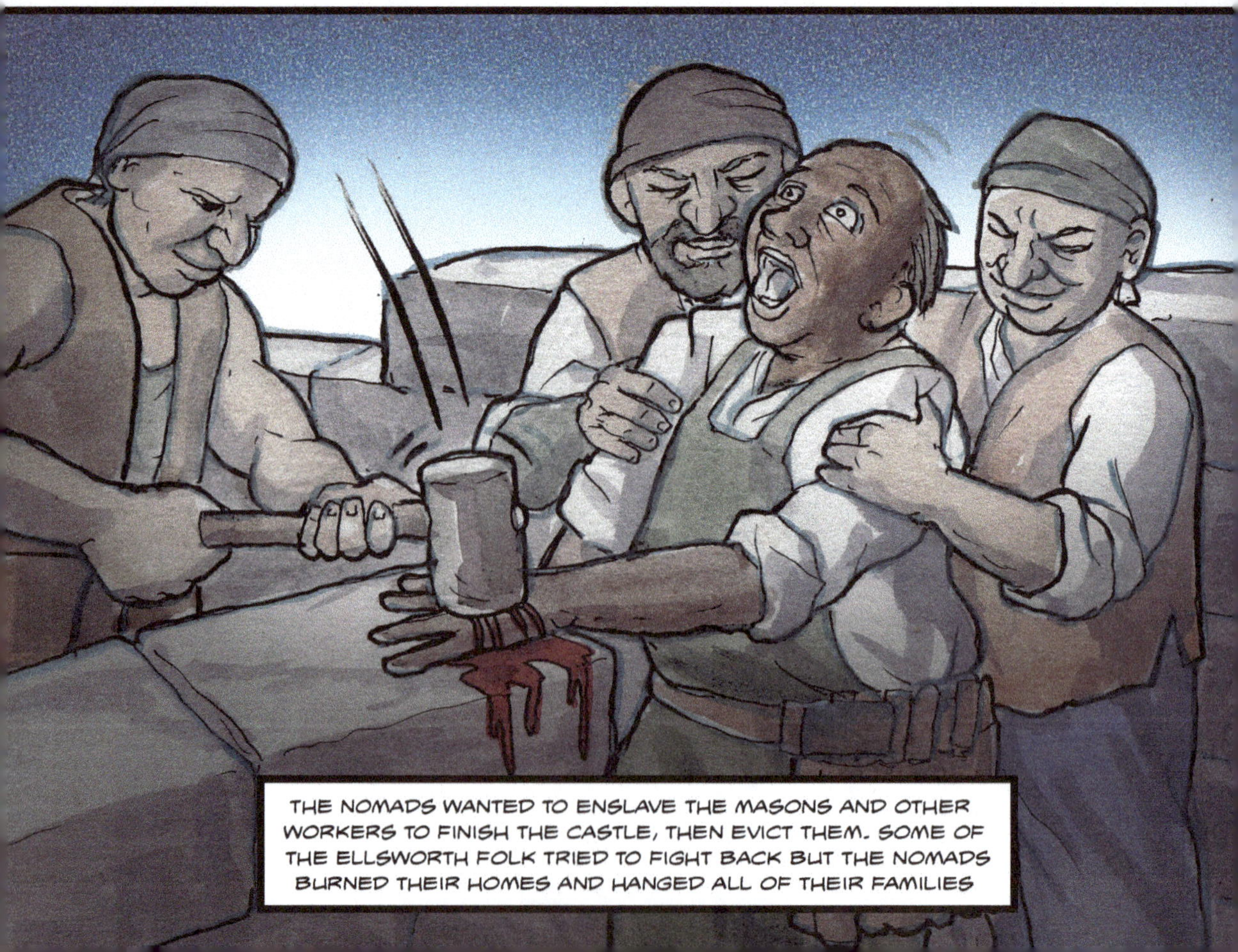

THE NOMADS WANTED TO ENSLAVE THE MASONS AND OTHER WORKERS TO FINISH THE CASTLE, THEN EVICT THEM. SOME OF THE ELLSWORTH FOLK TRIED TO FIGHT BACK BUT THE NOMADS BURNED THEIR HOMES AND HANGED ALL OF THEIR FAMILIES

PRAY CUT THEM DOWN
THEN I WENT TO SEE THE NOMADS TO DISCUSS THE RIGHTS OF THE LOCALS
EEEEEOOW

WACK!
WACK!
WACK!
WACK!
AFTER A LITTLE DISCUSSION I PERSUADED THEM TO TURN THEMSELVES INTO THE LOCAL ELLESWORTH GUARDS

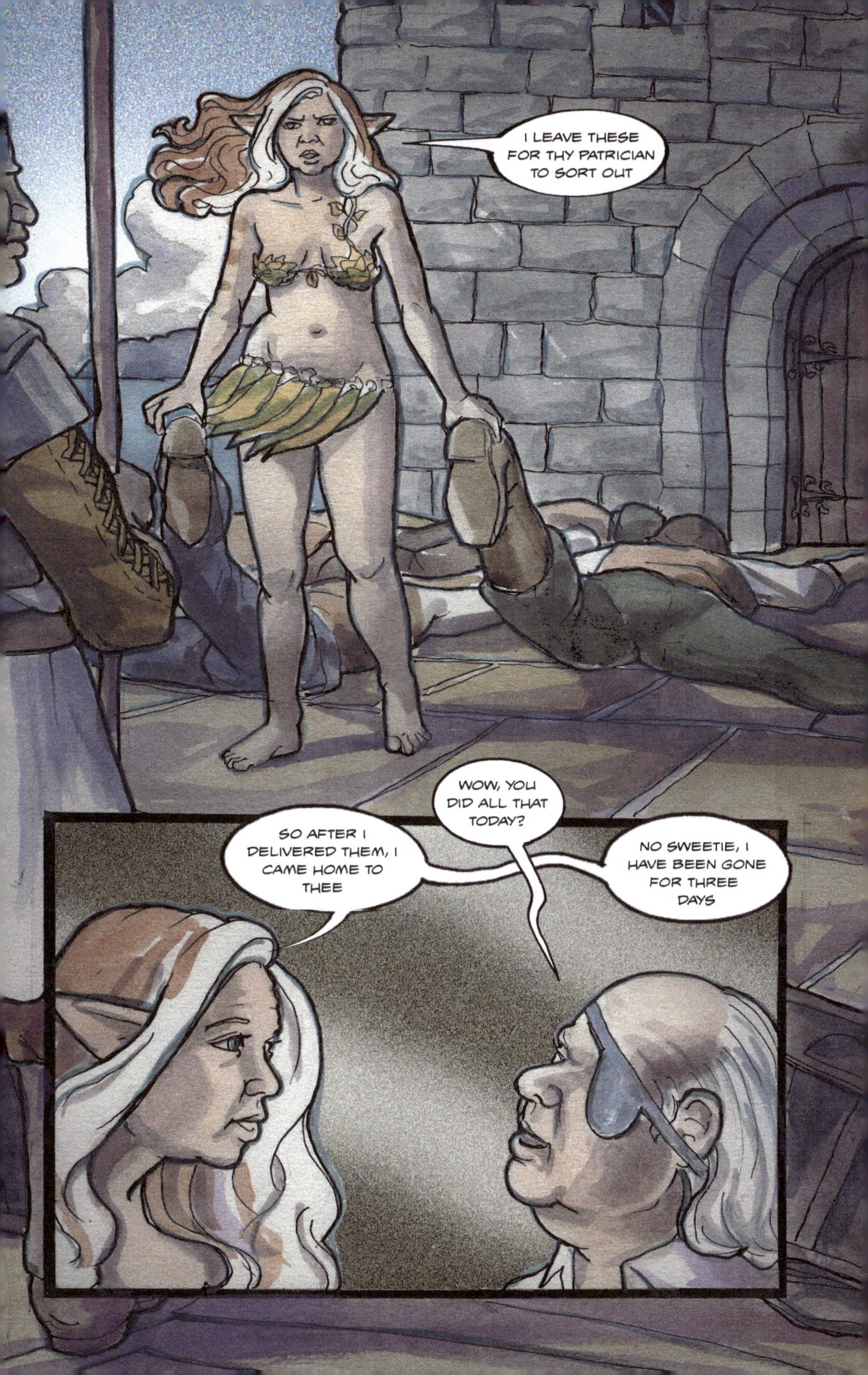

I LEAVE THESE FOR THY PATRICIAN TO SORT OUT
WOW, YOU DID ALL THAT TODAY?
SO AFTER I DELIVERED THEM, I CAME HOME TO THEE
NO SWEETIE, I HAVE BEEN GONE FOR THREE DAYS

I'M SORRY SHINE, I GET A BIT FUZZY AND FORGET THINGS
WORRY NOT MY LOVE, IT HAPPENS TO US ALL
HIIISSSS!
THERE BE NO POINT SCULKING, I KEN THOU ART THERE!
THY ATTENDANCE IS NOT NEEDED HERE, GET THEE HENCE
I AM SORRY SHINE OF THE MOON, I AM SURE YOU KNOW THAT DALE'S TIME IS NEAR, I HAVE COME TO EASE HIS PASSING

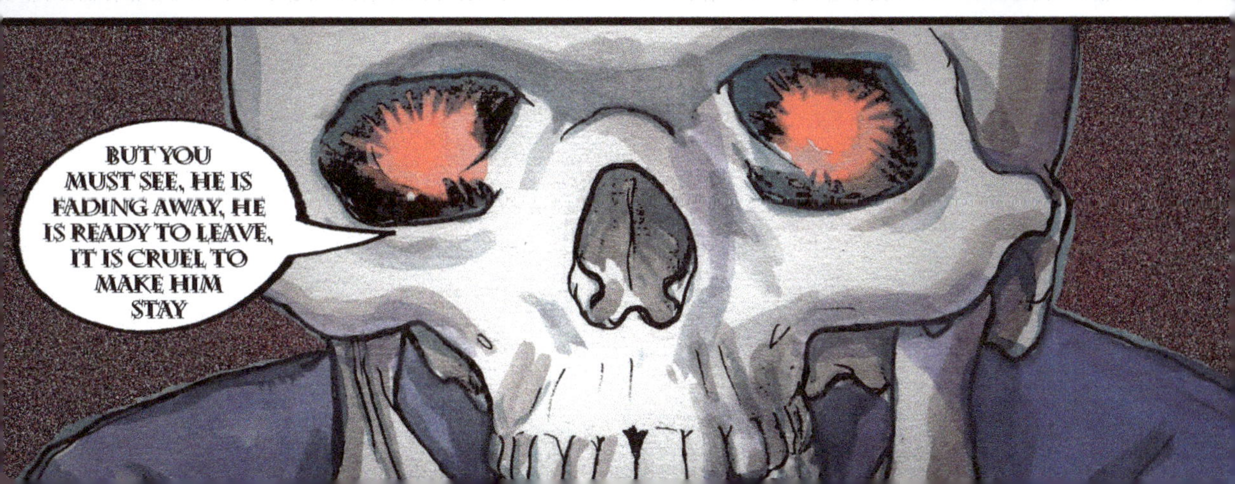
NO!
HE HAS COME TO THEE MANY TIMES AND I HAVE FETCHED HIM BACK
I WILL SAY WHEN IT IS HIS TIME!
BUT YOU MUST SEE, HE IS FADING AWAY, HE IS READY TO LEAVE, IT IS CRUEL TO MAKE HIM STAY

NOOO!
NO! I AM NOT READY FOR HIM TO GO
GO AWAY! I WILL BRING HIM TO THY KINGDOM MYSELF WHEN IT IS TIME
VERY WELL, BUT DO NOT DELAY TOO LONG, HE HAS COME TO HIS MORTAL ENDING

WEE MAGGIE?

AYE LASSIE?

PROTECT DALE! DEATH CAME FOR HIM BUT I WAS ABLE TO SEND HIM AWAY THIS TIME

GUID LASSIE, THAT SCUNNER CAN HAULD HEES HORSES, IF HE COMES BACK 'ERE I'LL CUT HEES BONEY LEGS FAE UNDER HIM. WHIT WULL YE DAE?

I GO TO SEE THE WIZARD, HE HAS LIVED FOR HUNDREDS OF YEARS, I NEED TO KNOW HOW!

YOU HAVEN'T HAD YOUR DINNER SWEETIE

I HAVE TO GO, WEE MAGGIE CAN HAVE MINE

PLEASE BE CAFEFUL LOOK AFTER YOURSELF

I KNOW I GET A BIT DOPEY AT TIMES BUT I STILL DO KNOW WHAT'S GOING ON. I KNOW MY TIME IS LIMITED AND I DON'T WANT YOU TO WORRY OR HURT YOURSELF TRYING TO FIX IT. I'VE HAD A GREAT LIFE WITH YOU AND I'M HAPPY
WE HAVE HAD A GREAT LIFE BUT GOBLINS LIVE MUCH LONGER THAN HUMANS AND I BE NAE READY FOR THEE TO LEAVE. I SHALL CHANGE THIS IF IT CAN BE CHANGED ... BUT... I WILL BE CAREFUL AND BE SAFE

WISZARD, THOU ART OLD I KEN THY AGE MUST BE OVER 200 YEARS, I NEED THIS ART FOR DALE
FOOLISH GOBLIN, I HAD TO STUDY FOR DECADES TO GAIN THIS KNOWLEDGE, TO BE ABLE TO PROLONG MY LIFE, DALE IS NEARLY DEAD, HE CAN'T LEARN WHAT HE NEEDS TO DO THIS!

THOU HAST MISSUNDERSTOOD ME, I DO NOT WANT DALE TO BECOME A WIIZARD
I WANT THEE TO GIVE DALE ANOTHER FIFTY YEARS!
OR IF THOU WISH TO TEST THY SPELLS I CAN SLIT THY GUT TO SEE IF THOU LIVES ON

VERY WELL! VERY WELL! I WILL GIVE YOU A POTION THAT WILL GIVE HIM AT LEAST 50 YEARS!
SEE! THAT WAS NAE HARD! IT BE SO MUCH NICER BEING A FRIEND AND HELPING 
THANK THEE SO VERY MUCH WIZARD, OH AND ... 
IF IT DOES NOT WORK I WILL COME BACK AND TEAR THY THROAT OUT

SCREEE

ZWOOSH

THUMP

YOU GOT HER, IS SHE THE RIGHT ONE?

SO WHO WAS SHE ANYWAY? WHAT WAS SHE?
SOME LOCAL HERO, A VIGILANTE, SHE TOOK OUT OUR WHOLE RAIDING PARTY
SHE DIDN'T SEEM THAT TOUGH, WHAT IS SHE ANYWAY? SOME SORT OF ANIMAL?
THAT'S IMPOSSIBLE, THERE WERE FIFTY GUYS IN THAT PARTY
IT'S TRUE! NOW THEY ARE HOLDING THEM HOSTAGE, THEY SAY WE HAVE NO RIGHT TO THIS LAND
NO RIGHT! HA! OUR ANCESTOR FIRST EXPLORED THIS LAND, IT IS OURS! WE ARE THE CHOSEN
CHOSEN OR NOT, RIGHT OR NOT, IT'S OUR LAND IF WE CAN TAKE IT AND WE CAN!

WHAT'S SHE GOT IN HER HAND? SHE'S HOLDING IT PRETTY TIGHT
I'LL TAKE IT, IT MIGHT BE VALUABLE
SNAP
SCRUNCH

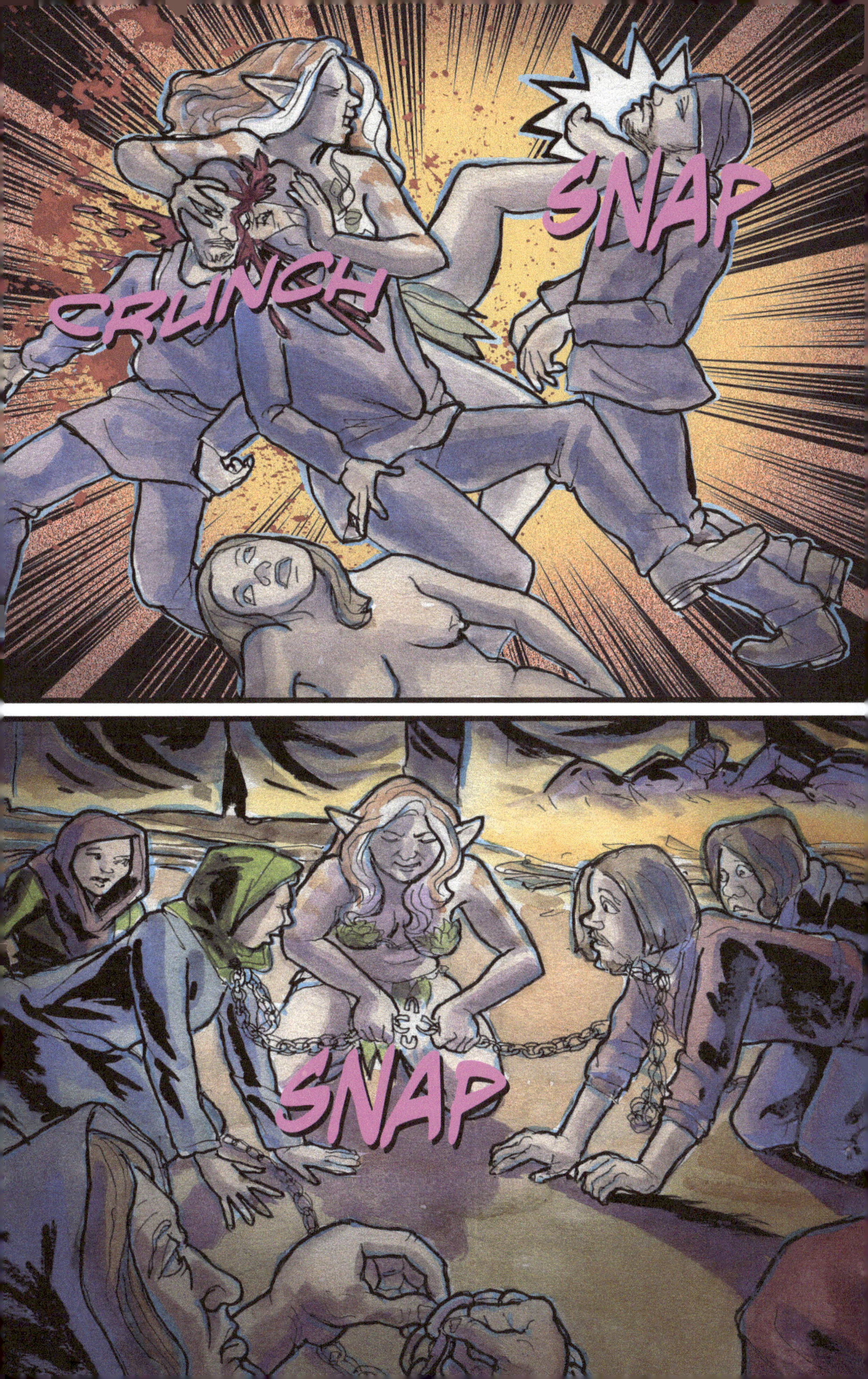

CRUNCH
SNAP

SNAP

ALL OF THEE WERE ON ONE CHAIN, THOU ART FREE! GO HOME BUT TAKE THY SISTER
SHE WAS ILL USED BY THESE MEN. BURY HER WHERE SHE CAN SEE HER HOME
WHO ARE YOU?
I AM ONE WHO IS NOT HAPPY WITH THY PEOPLE

MINE, I BELIEVE!
WHY DOST THOU DO THIS TO THE FOLK OF ELLSWORTH?
WE NEED A NEW HOMELAND, WE HAVE HISTORY WITH THIS LAND, WE HAVE THE RIGHT, WE HAVE GOD ON OUR SIDE
WHICH GOD?
JEHOVAH, THE ONLY TRUE GOD!
THESE FOLK BELIEVE IN THE SAME GOD AS THEE, THEY SHOULD BE THY FRIENDS

NO! WE ARE THE ONLY TRUE PEOPLE OF OUR GOD, WE CAN TRACE OUR FAITH BACK 4000 YEARS
I HAVE MET THY GOD, HE IS A SELFISH PETTY GOD. BUT WHY TRY TO KILL EVERYONE HERE? WHAT HAVE THEY DONE TO THEE?
WE HAVE BEEN PERSECUTED FOR EONS, NOW WE STRIKE FIRST! NEVER AGAIN A VICTIM
SO NOW THY WISH IS TO PERSECUTE THESE FOLK, TO MAKE THEM VICTIMS
YOU DON'T UNDERSTAND, THESE ARE NOT OF OUR PEOPLE, THEY DON'T MATTER, WE ARE MORE IMPORTANT, OUR SUFFERING IS GREATER THAN THEIRS
IF THESE ARE THE BELIEFS OF THY PEOPLE, THOU ART EVIL AND COVETOUS

WHAT ARE YOU DOING? WHERE ARE WE GOING?
IT BE NOT MY PLACE TO TREAT WITH THEE, I TAKE THEE TO ELLSWORTH
PATRICIAN, TWICE THY PREDECESSORS TRIED TO KILL ME, SO I HAVE NO LOVE FOR THEE BUT THOU NEEDEST TO SORT THIS MESS!
THIS IS THE NOMAD CHIEF GIVE HIS FOLK A NEW HOME! THE LAND TO THE WEST OF THY RIVER, KEEP THE COASTLANDS MAKE PEACE ERE THEE ALL DIE OF STUPIDITY
I LEAVE THEE TO SORT THIS OUT, DO IT IN GOOD FAITH OR I WILL BRING A THOUSAND GOBLINS AND TWO THOUSAND TROLLS TO SORT THEE OUT PERMANENTLY

THIS IS ALL TAKEN TOO LONG, I MUST GET BACK TO DALE

AYE YER SCUNNER, YE CANNA HAVE HIM
NOW MISS PIXIE, YOU KNOW HE IS BREATHING HIS LAST BREATHS
OCH AYE, BIT YET HE BREATHES AYE
I COULD KILL YOU WITH THE FLICK OF MY FINGER
AN' I CUID HAE YER BONEY HEID ROLLIN' O'ER TH' GROUND LIK' A FITBALL

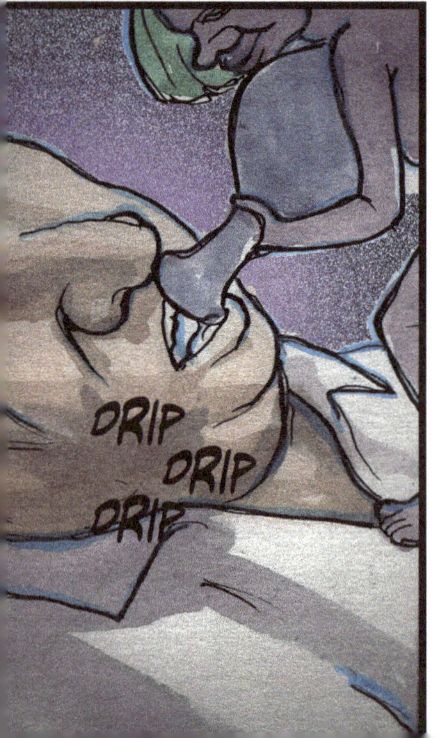

HISSS!
THIS IS NO PLACE FOR THEE

WEE MAGGIIE, PRAY GIVE THIS POTION TO DALE

DRIP
DRIP
DRIP

WELL DONE SHINE OF THE MOON, HE HAS SAND IN HIS TIMER AGAIN
DALE HAS 50 MORE YEARS, I CANNOT ASK THEE TO STAY SO LONG
AH WUL STAY, IT'S ME PROMISE YE KEN, AN' YE GUT A GOOD PUB HERE, AR'L STAY AND SMALL ANGUS WUL STA TOO
THANK YOU SHINE, YOU SAVED ME ... AGAIN, I FEEL YOUNG, BUT YOU KNOW THAT I CAN'T LIVE FOREVER
I'M SORRY I NEVER ASKED FOR THY WISHES, BUT THOU DOST NAE HAVE TO LIVE FOREVER, ...JUST FOR AS LONG AS I DO!

Shine of the Moon
Moon Rise
A GRAPHIC NOVEL BY JOHN LAWRY

Moon Shadow

THE COLLECTION
SHINE OF THE MOON
Volumes one, two and three
written and illustrated by John Lawry

SUN OF THE FOREST
A SHINE OF THE MOON STORY

Shine of the Moon
abnegation

SHINE OF THE MOON
CATACLYSM
A GRAPHIC NOVEL BY JOHN LAWRY

SHINE OF THE MOON
REVENANT
A GRAPHIC NOVEL BY JOHN LAWRY

SHINE OF THE MOON
METAMORPHOSIS
A GRAPHIC NOVEL BY JOHN LAWRY

MUTATIO
A GRAPHIC NOVEL BY JOHN LAWRY
FEATURING A SPECIAL GUEST APPEARANCE BY SHINE OF THE MOON

SHINE OF THE MOON
INCURSION

SHINE OF THE MOON
DEFIANCE
A GRAPHIC NOVEL BY JOHN LAWRY
FEATURING A SPECIAL GUEST APPEARANCE FROM
JOYCE'S CAVERN LIBRARY BY PETER LANE
CHAPTER TWO: CO-WRITTEN BY
JOHN LAWRY AND PETER LANE

SHINE OF THE MOON
COLONISATION
INCLUDING THE BONUS HOMECOMING
A SHINE OF THE MOON GRAPHIC NOVEL - BOOK 12
WRITTEN AND ILLUSTRATED BY JOHN LAWRY

SHINE OF THE MOON
THE GOD KILLER
WITH A BONUS LYN & ALEX STORY
CONTROL
TWO GRAPHIC NOVELLAS BY JOHN LAWRY

SHADOW & BREEZE
A GRAPHIC NOVEL SET IN SHINE OF THE MOON'S WORLD
WRITTEN AND ILLUSTRATED BY JOHN LAWRY

SHINE OF THE MOON
TALES
A SERIES OF SHORT STORIES FEATURING SHINE OF THE MOON
WRITTEN AND ILLUSTRATED BY JOHN LAWRY